James Mayhew
presents

Ella Bella
BALLERINA
~ and ~
The Sleeping Beauty

For Eloise
— Ella Bella —

Thanks to Liz Johnson and Tim Rose for their vision and inspiration,
and to Kate Burns for giving me the idea.
And thanks to Anglia Ruskin University in Cambridge
for offering a research grant.
J.M.

First edition for the United States, its territories and dependencies, and Canada
published in 2008 by Barron's Educational Series, Inc.

Text and illustrations © James Mayhew 2007

First published in 2007 by Orchard Books
338 Euston Road
London, NW1 3BH

All inquiries should be addressed to:
Barron's Educational Series, Inc.
250 Wireless Blvd.
Hauppauge, NY 11788
www.barronseduc.com

ISBN-13: 978-0-7641-6118-6
ISBN-10: 0-7641-6118-0

Library of Congress Catalog No.: 2007931490

Date of manufacture: August 2014
Manufactured by: South China Printing Co., Dongguan, China
9 8 7 6

James Mayhew
presents

Ella Bella
·BALLERINA·
~ and ~
The Sleeping Beauty

BARRON'S

Ella Bella loved Madame Rosa's ballet class
at the old theater.

The lessons were always fun. Ella Bella's favorite part was when they danced to the music from Madame Rosa's marvelous music box.

One day, Madame Rosa said,
"My darlings, let us listen to the music
from *The Sleeping Beauty* ballet.
I want you all to imagine
you are fairies!"

Madame Rosa opened the box and sparkly music filled the air. The little ballerina inside the box began to twirl, and Ella Bella and her friends danced like pretty fairies.

"Please tell us the story of Sleeping Beauty," said Ella Bella.

"Well," said Madame Rosa, "her name
was Princess Aurora and she was born
in a fairytale palace . . . "

"Princess Aurora's christening was a joyous event. Good fairies gathered and bestowed gifts of beauty and grace. But then, disaster! The bad fairy arrived. Furious not to be invited to the palace, she cast an evil spell – on her sixteenth birthday, Aurora would prick her finger on a spindle and die!"

"How terrible!" gasped the children.
"Ah, but the kind Lilac Fairy still had a gift to give," smiled Madame Rosa. "She changed the spell so that Aurora wouldn't die, but would sleep for a hundred years, only to be woken by a prince's kiss!"
"And did the prince come?" asked Ella Bella.

"My dear, there isn't time
for the whole story today,"
smiled Madame Rosa, closing
the music box. "It's nearly
time to go home."

The other children went to
get their coats, but Ella Bella
stayed behind on the stage . . .

When she was all
alone, Ella Bella
opened the music box.
Just like magic, the
music started and
Ella Bella found she
was dancing . . .

The music seemed to surround Ella Bella, and
then a tiny lilac light lit the music box.
It grew brighter and brighter until
Ella Bella saw a fairy floating toward her!

"I'm the Lilac Fairy," she smiled. "Shall we go?"
"Go where?" gasped Ella Bella.
"To Princess Aurora's sixteenth birthday party,
of course," said the Lilac Fairy.

The Lilac Fairy led Ella Bella
into a palace garden, and there
was Princess Aurora!

As she danced, everyone agreed that she
had grown to be the most beautiful princess
they'd ever seen. But then an old woman
shuffled out of the shadows with a gift for
Aurora – a spindle!

Ella Bella remembered the bad fairy's spell.
"Don't touch it!" she called.

But Aurora didn't hear.
She graciously took the
spindle and danced.

Suddenly, she
pricked her finger!

Aurora's dance became
faster and faster,

until she fell
to the floor!

The old woman threw off her cloak. It was
the bad fairy! She vanished in a flash before
anyone could catch her.

"Carry Aurora to the tallest tower," said
the Lilac Fairy sadly. "There she will sleep
for one hundred years."

"But what about everyone else?" wondered
Ella Bella.

"We'll put a spell on them, too," whispered
the Lilac Fairy.

Ella Bella took the Lilac Fairy's
hand and they began to fly.
It was like dancing in the air!
They sprinkled a spell over
the whole palace, and soon
everyone had fallen fast asleep.

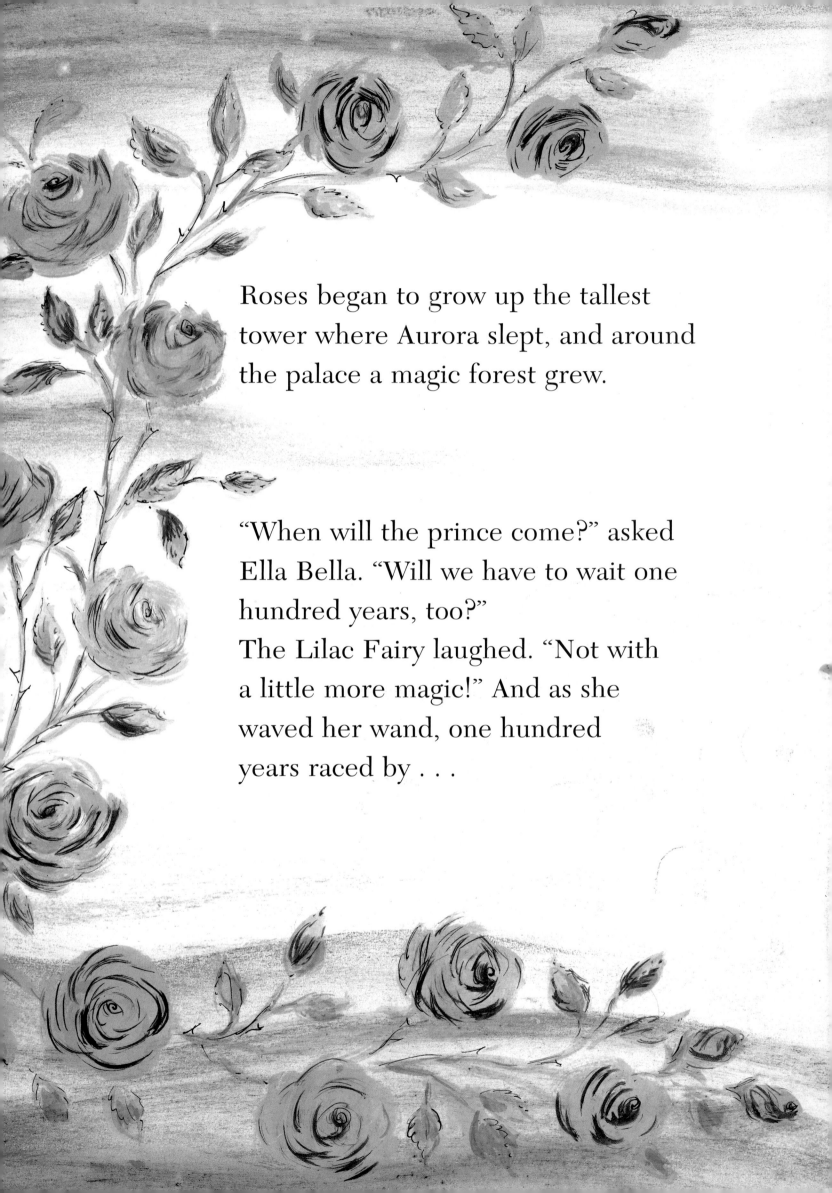

Roses began to grow up the tallest
tower where Aurora slept, and around
the palace a magic forest grew.

"When will the prince come?" asked
Ella Bella. "Will we have to wait one
hundred years, too?"
The Lilac Fairy laughed. "Not with
a little more magic!" And as she
waved her wand, one hundred
years raced by . . .

Ella Bella saw they were now in another kingdom. A dashing prince was riding toward them. The Lilac Fairy told him the sad tale of Princess Aurora, asleep in the tower.

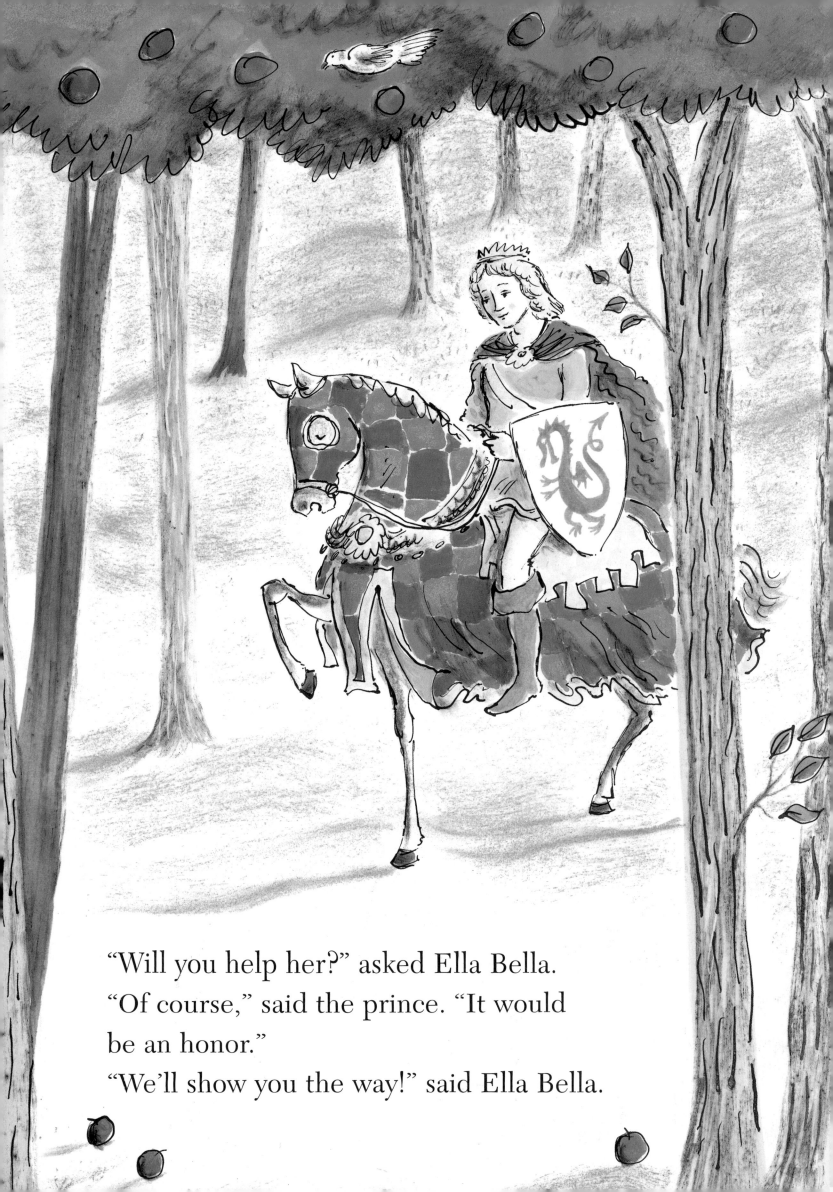

"Will you help her?" asked Ella Bella.
"Of course," said the prince. "It would
be an honor."
"We'll show you the way!" said Ella Bella.

They led the prince to the magic forest. He
slashed through the rosebushes with his gleaming
sword. Even though the thorns tore at him, he
didn't stop until he found Aurora's tower.

Gently, he kissed Aurora, and slowly,
softly she opened her eyes and smiled.
It was love at
first sight.

As soon as Aurora awoke, the magic forest
vanished and the whole palace leapt back to life.
"I love it when my spells work," said the
Lilac Fairy. "Let's take a peek at their wedding!"

What a wedding it was!
There was music and feasting, with guests
from all corners of the fairytale kingdom!
"Thank you for your help," said the Lilac Fairy.
"Now they will live happily ever after!"

"Thank you for a magical time!"
said Ella Bella.
The Lilac Fairy lifted her
wand once more and
the palace was filled with
lilac light and swirling music . . .

Then suddenly the music stopped,
and Ella Bella found herself alone
on the dark stage. She gently closed
the lid of the music box.

"There you are!" said Madame Rosa, giving
Ella Bella her cape. "Your mother is waiting."
"Can we listen to your music box next time?"
asked Ella Bella.
"Of course," said Madame Rosa. "We'll play
a different tune, shall we?"
"I'd like that!" said Ella Bella.

And, humming as she went, Ella Bella danced
with her mother all the way home.

The Sleeping Beauty is one of the most popular ballets. It was first performed in 1890 at the magnificent Mariinsky Theatre in St. Petersburg, Russia. Many spectacular ballets were created there, and their dazzling Russian dancers became famous all over the world.

The music for *The Sleeping Beauty*, written by Piotr Tchaikovsky, is full of glorious melodies, some of which are very well known.

It is exciting to go to the ballet. The music, played by an orchestra, and the theater, stage sets, and costumes are often very beautiful. But it is the dancers that really bring magic and wonder to the performances. They have to work incredibly hard, dancing each step perfectly to tell the story in exactly the right way. Every step, expression, and hand movement has a different meaning and so it is possible to tell a story without any words being spoken. Tchaikovsky's music also helps to tell the tale.

The Sleeping Beauty ballet is based on the story *The Beauty in the Sleeping Forest*, an old French fairy tale by Charles Perrault. Tchaikovsky liked fairy tales so much that he added some other characters to Princess Aurora's wedding, including Cinderella and her prince, Hop-o-My-Thumb, Puss-in-Boots, The Blue Bird, and even Little Red Riding Hood, who dances with a wolf! Did you spot them in the wedding picture earlier in the book?